THE HEIGHTS

SAIL

SADDLEBACK
EDUCATIONAL PUBLISHING

THE HEIGHTS

Blizzard	River
Camp	**Sail**
Crash	Score
Dive	Swamp
Neptune	Twister

Original text by Ed Hansen
Adapted by Mary Kate Doman

SADDLEBACK
EDUCATIONAL PUBLISHING
www.sdlback.com

ISBN-13: 978-1-61651-622-2
ISBN-10: 1-61651-622-4
eBook: 978-1-61247-307-9

Printed in Guangzhou, China
0611/CA21100644

16 15 14 13 12   1 2 3 4 5 6

Chapter 1

Antonio and Lilia were alone. They just got home from school. The phone rang. Antonio ran to get it. But Lilia ran past him. She answered the phone.

"Hey, Dad!" Lilia said.

"Hi, Lilia," said Rafael. "What's going on?"

"Not much. Antonio and I just got home," said Lilia. "When will your work be done?"

"It's a big job. I'll be gone a while," said Rafael.

Antonio took the phone from Lilia.

"Dad! Wassup?" asked Antonio.

"Hi, Antonio. Remind me. Is school finished next week?" Rafael asked.

"Yes. Six days and counting," said Antonio.

"Great," Rafael said. "I want to take you all on a trip."

"Cool. Where?" Antonio asked.

"We're going to sail around the Bahamas. I rented a sail boat in Miami," said Rafael.

Lilia and Antonio were excited. They had all been sailing before. They talked about the plan for a few more minutes. Rafael had to get back to work.

"Do you think Mom will come?" Lilia asked Antonio.

"Doubt it," Antonio said. "She doesn't like to travel."

"Yeah," said Lilia. "She stays in the Heights."

Rafael said that they would leave from Miami. Then sail for two weeks.

That night he booked three plane tickets. Ana was staying in the Heights. But Rafael loved taking his kids on vacation.

Ana Silva drove her kids to the airport. She hugged them good-bye. Then she told them to have a great time.

"And give your dad a big hug from me," Ana said. "I miss him when he works on these big jobs. Maybe I'll surprise you at the end of the trip."

Rafael was in Miami. He met his kids at the airport. The Silva kids got off the plane. They went to get their bags. Rafael waved to them. Lilia saw him first. She ran up to him.

"Hi, Daddy!" Lilia yelled.

Rafael smiled. He gave her a big hug. Antonio and Franco hugged him too.

"This is going to be sweet," said Antonio.

"Yes, it is," Rafael said. "We're sailing all over the Bahamas. We'll swim, fish, and sail. Franco, I hope you remember how to sail. I'm going to need your help. Our boat is 42 feet!"

"No problem, Dad. I remember," Franco said.

"Great! Let's get your bags," Rafael said. "Then we'll go to the boat."

The boat was called the *Sea Mist*. It was blue and white. She looked sleek and fast. Lilia looked up and up. She couldn't believe how tall the mast was.

"Wow, Dad! The boat is huge! It's like 100 feet tall," said Lilia.

Rafael laughed. "Well, it's not that big! But it's tall," Rafael said. "Let's go on board. I'll show you around."

They all boarded the *Sea Mist*.

Rafael pointed. "This is where we steer the boat," he said. "That wheel controls the rudder."

Next, they went into a small room. It was the wheelhouse. A table was covered with maps.

Then they went below. It was cramped. There were three little cabins where they would sleep. A kitchen was there too.

"Franco and Lilia, put everything away," Rafael said. "Antonio and I will go to the store. Any requests?"

"Peanut butter," Lilia said. "Don't forget the peanut butter."

"And frozen pizza," said Franco.

"Do you ever eat good food?" Rafael asked.

"Only when Mom makes us," said Franco.

Rafael laughed. "Forget it. I'll pick out the food. We're going to be working hard. You'll get hungry," he said.

At the store, Rafael filled two carts with food. They would be at sea for 12 days. And there were a lot of mouths to feed. Antonio put frozen pizza, cookies, and candy in the cart.

"That's enough junk food," Rafael said.

"Dad, we're on vacation," said Antonio. "You sound like Mom."

They got back to the boat before dark. And they put the food away. Rafael checked his list:

Food ✓
Fresh water—160 gallons ✓
Gas—100 gallons ✓
Fishing gear ✓
Diving gear ✓

Sleeping gear ✓
Flashlight ✓
Radio ✓

"There's one rule, kids," Rafael said. "Everyone has to wear a life jacket on deck. Got that? Okay! Now we're ready. We ship out tomorrow morning."

Chapter 2

They took off at 6 o'clock. It was time to start the trip. Franco helped his father. Antonio and Lilia were still asleep. The *Sea Mist* motored away from land. Rafael used the engine. In open water, he'd use the sail.

Soon, they were clear of land. Franco was ready to raise the sail.

"Take her up, Franco," Rafael said.

Franco raised the sail. Rafael turned off the motor. The only sounds were the wind and splashing water. It was nice and peaceful. Then Lilia came up on deck.

"Why didn't you wake me up?" Lilia asked.

"We have a lot of work to do. I wanted you to rest up," said Rafael.

The *Sea Mist* was going five knots. They'd been at sea for two hours. The coast was far away.

Rafael set a course for Grand Bahama Island. It was 100 miles away. They'd get there the next morning.

At 8:30 a.m., Rafael was hungry.

"Hey, Lilia, want to make us some breakfast?" Rafael asked.

"Antonio can make breakfast. I want to learn how to sail," said Lilia.

Lilia took the wheel. Rafael showed her how to steer. Then he showed her how to use a compass. Water was all around. They couldn't see any land. Without a compass, they'd be lost.

"The *Sea Mist* is all yours now," Rafael said. "I'm going to check on the boys."

Lilia was happy. She was alone on the deck. She was sailing!

Rafael went to the kitchen. The boys were cooking.

"Who's steering the boat?" Antonio asked.

"Lilia," said Rafael.

"Dad! Lilia is young!" Antonio

yelled. "She can't sail."

"Yes, she can. She's sailing right now," Rafael said. "By the end of the week, she'll be a pro."

The rest of the day was great. Each Silva steered the boat. The wind was strong. It was perfect.

The Silvas sailed all night. They took turns sleeping. Someone had to steer at all times. The night was beautiful. They could see so many stars.

In the morning, they anchored the boat. They were in the Bahamas! Everyone put on bathing suits. Soon they were in the water. They explored around the boat. All they needed were masks and snorkels.

Later that afternoon, they swam

to a little beach. Rafael and Lilia sat on the sand. Antonio and Franco explored the island. They'd been at sea for two days. It was nice to walk around. Rafael made dinner on the beach. It was a great day.

"I like it here. Can we stay another day?" Antonio asked.

The Silvas voted. Everyone else wanted to stay too. So they spent another day on the beach.

The Abaco Islands were their next stop. To get there they would have to sail all night.

Rafael and Antonio steered the boat. Franco and Lilia slept. Franco would steer at 1 a.m. It was a calm night.

The night was dark. There was a

red light in the distance.

"What's that light?" asked Antonio.

"It's another boat. But it's far away," said Rafael. "The *Sea Mist* has one too. All boats have two lights. They all have a red and a green one. It's so boaters see each other."

"Cool," said Antonio. "I never knew that before."

One o'clock came fast. Franco came on deck. He was ready to sail.

"Wake me if there's a problem. If not, I'll be up at 6 o'clock," said Rafael.

Franco liked the sea at night. He thought about football. Practice was starting in August. He was excited.

Time flew by. Soon, Rafael was on deck.

"Morning, Franco. Have you seen the island yet?" Rafael asked.

"I just saw it," answered Franco.

"Great!" said Rafael. "There's a little cove over there." Rafael pointed. "We'll spend the afternoon there. Later we'll go into town."

Rafael dropped anchor. The Silvas swam all day. The water was warm. It was beautiful. There were so many colorful fish.

"This is much better than school," Antonio said. Everyone laughed. They all agreed.

Chapter 3

The Silvas stayed in the cove. The next day they'd go to town. The town was called Marsh Harbour.

Rafael lay in bed. He thought about this great trip. Everyone was having fun. "Sailing at night is fun," Rafael thought. "But it's hard to get sleep!"

They were off early the next day. Lilia pulled up the anchor. Franco sailed the boat to Marsh Harbour. It was only 40 miles away. But it took all day to get there.

The *Sea Mist* got to Marsh Harbour at 6 o'clock. That night they went out to dinner. It was nice to eat on dry land.

Rafael wanted to leave Marsh Harbour early tomorrow. The longest part of the trip was next. They were sailing to Nassau. It was 200 miles away.

"Let's call your mom," Rafael said.

"Yeah! She'll be happy to hear from us," Lilia said.

Everyone took turns talking to Ana. Rafael spoke to her last. He told her how great everything was. He told her he wished she was with them. They both smiled.

The *Sea Mist* left for Nassau the next day. They were sailing the open sea. It was awesome! But the weather was strange.

Rafael checked the weather report. He got scared at what he heard. A loud voice on the radio said, "A storm is coming. All boats avoid the open sea. High winds and rough water expected."

The *Sea Mist* was heading into a storm! Rafael was worried. He'd been in storms before. It wasn't fun. Storms were dangerous. Bad storms could be deadly.

Maybe the storm would change direction. They may be able to miss the worst of it. But the radio reported a hurricane watch. The storm was growing stronger!

Rafael was really worried. He knew the boat couldn't outrun the storm. But he had to try. Rafael went up on the deck. He told Franco to turn around. He hoped that the *Sea Mist* was very fast!

Chapter 4

Rain started to fall. The wind picked up. Lightning lit up the sky.

Then, sparks flew from the radio.

"Oh, no!" Rafael thought. "Did lightning strike our radio?"

Rafael looked at the radio. Smoke was coming out of it. It smelled like it was burning. The worst had happened. The radio was gone!

Antonio and Lilia came on deck.

"What's going on?" Lilia asked. "Why is the water so rough?"

"A storm's coming," Rafael said. "I need your help. Put on your life jackets. Don't take them off, no matter what happens!"

The kids could tell Rafael was worried. They did what he said.

"Antonio and Lilia go below. Tie down everything that can move. Franco, steer the boat. Keep us on course."

The waves were over eight feet. Rafael had to take the sail down. It wasn't easy. The wind and rain were strong. But he finally got it down. Then he turned on the engine.

The waves tossed the boat. It was hard to move. Rafael told Antonio and Lilia to stay below deck. He didn't want them to fall overboard.

They made it through the night. No one slept. And the storm was worse. The winds were 50 miles per hour. The waves were 20 feet high. And it rained harder than before. The *Sea Mist* was in the middle of a hurricane. Rafael sighed. He wished he never brought his kids on this trip.

Then a huge wave hit the *Sea Mist*. It knocked off the wheelhouse. The crash made a hole in the deck! There was no way to fix it. Water was everywhere. The *Sea Mist* was sinking!

"This is it," thought Rafael. "The *Sea Mist* is sinking. It's sinking fast. We have to get off."

"We're going in the life raft," yelled Rafael. "Grab anything you can. Do it fast!"

Rafael untied the raft. Lilia and Antonio ran to the deck. Each had their arms full of food and supplies. All four Silvas climbed on the raft. They were free of the sinking boat.

Rafael told the kids to tie themselves to the raft. A big wave hit. Lilia fell into the water.

"Daddy!" Lilia screamed.

Then she disappeared.

Chapter 5

Franco saw Lilia fall overboard. He jumped in after her.

"No, Franco! Franco!" Rafael shouted.

But Franco didn't hear him. The storm was too loud. Rafael couldn't see anything. Two of his kids were gone!

Then Rafael saw something. It was a life jacket! Franco held on to

Lilia. Rafael steered the raft to his kids. He pulled them into the raft. Then he secured them. He didn't want them to fall out again.

"Franco, that's the bravest thing I ever saw," said Rafael. "You saved your sister's life! I don't know how to thank you."

"I do, Dad," Franco said. "Remember this when I get my driver's license. You can get me a car! Well, only if we make it."

"We'll make it," Rafael said. "We'll talk about the car later."

Rafael looked around. Almost all of their supplies were gone. All they had was a survival kit. It wasn't much.

Rafael made a mental list.

Inside the kit was a canvas tarp. Some canned food. A pint of fresh water. A fishhook and line. A flare gun with three flares. Some matches. A pocketknife. A flashlight. That was it.

Rafael knew things were bad. They were far from land. They had very little food and water. But that wasn't the worst thing. Not having a radio was the worst. They couldn't call for help. No one would look for them. No one even knew the *Sea Mist* had sunk. The Silvas were lost at sea!

Everyone was tired. They moved close together for warmth. Then they fell asleep. But Antonio woke up. He had an idea. He thought it might help them.

First, Antonio took off his rubber rain pants. He tied the legs together. Next, he tied the pants to a paddle. The pants hung like a flag. They filled up with rainwater. But it took a long time. Antonio's arms hurt. The paddle got heavy. But he knew they needed water.

Chapter 6

Everyone woke at dawn. They were all cold.

"We don't have to worry about drinking water," Antonio said.

"Yes, we do," Rafael said. "We don't have much."

"No, I collected water all night. I got a lot," said Antonio.

Franco looked puzzled. "What? How did you do that?" asked Franco.

Antonio told them what he did. Rafael was amazed.

"What a great idea!" said Rafael. "You really helped us."

"I know," Antonio said. "And Dad, in five years, you can get me a car too!"

Rafael smiled. His kids were amazing. He couldn't believe how smart they were.

"I'm not drinking water from Antonio's pants! That's gross!" Lilia said.

Rafael and the boys laughed.

The storm was 40 miles away. The seas were getting quiet. It stopped raining. Everyone was wet, cold, and hungry. They were going to have a hard day.

The sea between the Bahamas and Florida was busy. Rafael hoped they would be rescued soon. They ate some of the food from the survival kit. No one spoke much.

At noon, Franco heard a noise. "Look! A plane," he yelled.

Everyone looked up.

"He has to see us! Give me the flare gun," Rafael yelled.

Rafael fired the gun. The flare shot into the sky. But the plane didn't turn around.

"What's wrong with that pilot? Didn't he see our flare?" asked Lilia.

"Don't worry. Someone else will see it," Rafael said.

Rafael was mad that the plane didn't see them. But he didn't want his kids to know. He knew it was important to stay calm. They floated in the raft the rest of the day.

Dinner was kit food. Stars were out. The night was nice. But the wind was cold. They were all tired again. Everyone quickly fell asleep.

Chapter 7

The next morning, the sun was bright. It felt good. It had been a long time since everyone was warm. But Rafael knew that too much sun was bad. They had no hats or sunscreen. Rafael put the tarp up for shade. He hoped it worked.

Lilia was bored. Franco told her to try fishing. She thought it was a great idea. Lilia got a line and a hook.

But she didn't have any bait. So she made her own bait. She put an empty can on the hook. It was shiny. She thought it would attract fish.

Lilia dropped the line in the water. Then she tied the end around her arm. She waited for a bite. But nothing happened. Before long she fell asleep.

A big tug on the line woke up Lilia.

"I've got a bite!" Lilia yelled.

Everyone looked at Lilia. She pulled up the line.

"It's a big one!" Lilia yelled.

Franco helped her pull. Lilia caught a tuna!

Rafael was excited. Raw fish wasn't their favorite food. But it was something good for them to eat.

"Good job, Lilia," Antonio said. "I got us water. You got us fish!"

Rafael cleaned the fish. He threw the head and bones in the water. Antonio watched. Then he saw something under the water. He couldn't believe his eyes!

"Shark!" Antonio yelled.

Rafael looked down. To his shock, he saw the shark. It headed right for the raft. Rafael knew the shark would tear the raft apart.

"We have to keep it away from the raft! Franco, grab a paddle. Help me fight it off," Rafael yelled.

The fin disappeared. But then it came up next to the raft. The raft tipped to one side. Rafael and Franco hit the shark with the paddle. The shark swam away. Then it turned and swam to the raft again. Lilia was crying.

Again and again, the shark hit the raft. Again and again, Rafael and Franco hit the shark. It kept coming back.

The shark lifted its head out of the water. Rafael brought the paddle down hard. He hit the shark on its nose. The shark swam away. This time it didn't come back.

"That had to hurt!" Antonio said.

"I hope so," said Rafael. "I hope it's gone for good."

The Silvas watched the water. The fin never came back.

At night they heard an airplane. The kids yelled and waved. Rafael fired the second flare. It flew up into the air. But the plane flew by. Everyone was quiet the rest of the night. They were too scared to talk.

Chapter 8

The sun rose early. Rafael woke up in a bad mood. He was losing hope. He was afraid they wouldn't get rescued. But he had to stay strong.

They hadn't seen a boat since the storm. They were running out of food and water. Only one flare was left. Things couldn't get much worse.

Everyone was scared. Lilia thought about her mom. She didn't know if she'd ever see her again.

Antonio thought about his mom too. "I wonder if she knows we're lost," he thought.

Franco wasn't as worried. He thought they'd get rescued. He wanted it to be today. But if not today, they'd be rescued tomorrow. Football practice started in a few days. He had to be home for that!

Rafael also thought about Ana. He thought about how different they were. He loved adventure. She loved the Heights. Maybe she was right?

But Rafael liked to travel. He'd already worked in 24 countries. And he was very well paid. Should he give that up? He thought about a teaching job. Ana begged him to do that.

"Money is not the most important thing," Ana said.

Rafael missed Ana. But right now he had to save them all.

The day went by slowly. There were no new problems. As soon as it was dark, everyone fell asleep.

It was before dawn! Antonio woke up. The raft bobbed up and down. Antonio looked over the side of the raft. He thought he saw something. But it was still dark.

He looked harder. Yes! He was sure now. It was a red light. It had to be a boat! But it was going past them. There was no time to waste. Antonio grabbed the flare gun. And he fired the last flare into the sky.

Chapter 9

A huge cruise ship headed to Miami. First Officer Ruiz was on deck. He'd gotten a report. The night watchman saw a flare. Ruiz looked up. He didn't see anything. But he couldn't be sure. He notified the captain.

Captain Turner answered the call. Ruiz told him about the flare.

"Did you see it?" the captain asked.

"No, sir, but the watchman did," Ruiz said.

"Okay, let's check it out. Turn the ship around," said the captain. "I'll be there soon."

"Yes, sir," Ruiz answered.

Antonio woke his father. He told him what he'd done. Rafael was worried. He thought Antonio wasted the last flare.

Rafael looked where Antonio saw the light. Rafael saw red and green lights. Antonio was right! That could only mean one thing. The ship turned around. Now it headed toward them.

They were finally getting a break. Rafael had to make sure the ship could see them.

He told Antonio to grab the flashlight. Antonio handed it to his dad. But nothing happened when Rafael turned it on. The batteries were dead.

Everyone on the ship looked for a flare. They couldn't see anything.

Finally the captain sighed.

"I guess it was a false alarm. Let's head back," said Captain Turner.

The huge ship turned around. The lights were gone. Rafael's mind raced.

"What more can I do?" Rafael yelled. "Please—don't leave!"

Then he remembered the matches. Rafael tore off his shirt. He tied it around a paddle.

Rafael lit five matches. The shirt

finally caught fire. He waved the paddle back and forth.

"Please! Please look back," yelled Rafael. The night watchman saw the fire. He ran to the captain.

"There's something out there, sir. Look!" the night watchman yelled.

Captain Turner looked. This time he saw the Silvas!

"Full stop! Mr. Ruiz, turn on the searchlights," the captain said.

The ship was huge. And the searchlights were bright. Everyone on the raft waved to the big ship.

Finally, they heard a voice. "Hold on!" said the voice. "We're lowering a boat for you."

Tears rolled down Rafael's face. He hugged his children. He'd never been happier!

Captain Turner greeted the Silvas.

"How long were you out there?" Captain Turner asked.

"Four days. Maybe five," said Rafael. "We lost track of time."

Captain Turner was shocked!

Mr. Ruiz got the Silvas dry clothes. He also showed them where they could take hot showers.

Rafael thanked him. Then he took a long, hot shower.

Captain Turner ordered pizza from the kitchen. Rafael told the crew about their days on the raft. The crew couldn't believe the story. The Silvas couldn't believe how good the pizza tasted!

Chapter 10

The cruise ship docked in Miami.
The Silvas thanked the captain and
crew.

Rafael booked a hotel room. They
were spending the rest of their trip
on land.

Rafael knew he had to call Ana.
But he was not looking forward to
it. She was not going to like what
happened. She'd be happy they were

safe. But she would be mad that he didn't check the weather report earlier.

Lilia wanted to call her mom. So Rafael let her make the call. Lilia told her mom everything. Rafael and the boys heard Ana yelling. Then Lilia gave Rafael the phone. She gave her dad a shrug.

"Uh-oh," Rafael thought. "This will be worse than being lost at sea!" And he was right!